Library Learning Information

Idea Store®
Whitechapel
321 Whitechapel Road
London E1 1BU

020 7364 4332
www.ideastore.co.uk

Created and managed by
Tower Hamlets Council

Published by the Cool*Books* Project: a partnership between Gatehouse
Publishing Charity Ltd and the Writers in Prison *Network*,
c/o Gatehouse Books Ltd, Hulme Adult Education Centre, Stretford
Road, Manchester, M15 5FQ

Editors for Gatehouse, Patricia Duffin, Stella Fitzpatrick.
Writer in Residence at HMYOI Glen Parva, Gareth Creer.
Illustrations and cover design, Ivor Arbuckle
Printed by RAP Ltd, Oldham

The Cool*Books* Project is grateful for the support of Governors and staff
at HMP/YOI Foston Hall, HMYOI Glen Parva, HMP/YOI Styal Prison and
HMYOI Swinfen Hall and for their opinions and comments to the
prisoners and staff who made up the Reading Circles, who
recommended this book for publication.

Special thanks to HMYOI Hindley for additional support towards the end
of the project.

The Cool*Books* Project is grateful for financial support from DCMS/
Wolfson Public Libraries Challenge Fund and Prison Regime Services

It all started as a joke

John Tuff

Cool*Books*

Gatehouse Books

Books by and for adult learners

The **Cool*Books*** pilot project is a partnership between The Gatehouse Publishing Charity and The Writers in Prison *Network*. Writing workshops aimed at prisoners with basic skills needs were set up and co-run by Writers in residence and Gatehouse staff using a range of methods to stimulate and develop writing. The writing was then passed to *reading circles* which again comprised prisoners with basic skills needs. The groups met over several sessions to choose the texts which would go forward for piloting as a book.

There are 6 pilot publications in total.

Who are Gatehouse?

Gatehouse is a unique Manchester based community publisher. We have been publishing books for adults with reading and writing

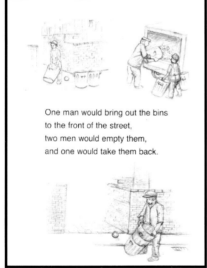

One man would bring out the bins
to the front of the street,
two men would empty them,
and one would take them back.

difficulties for the past 23 years. Uniquely in publishing, Gatehouse authors are themselves adult learners who are developing their reading and writing skills. At Gatehouse we believe that the best people to write for adult learners are those who have been through the same experience themselves. So Gatehouse books speak of an experience that readers can understand and share. If you enjoyed this book then we are sure you will enjoy many of the Gatehouse titles.

extract from 'The Bin Men'

Booklist Available

Gatehouse Books
Hulme Adult Education Centre
Stretford Road
Manchester M15 5FQ
Tel: 0161 226 7152
E-mail: office@gatehousebooks.org.uk
www.gatehousebooks.org.uk

Introduction

My story is dedicated
to all those who feel life is empty.
My story is about a hostage situation
that went wrong.

I was born in 1981 in Leicester.
From the age of fifteen I've been in trouble
and spent the best part in YOI's since.
Don't waste your life.
Grass isn't always greener on the other side,
as I found out.

I hope you can relate
to what is going on in this book
and enjoy.

John Tuff

It all started as a joke.

We were planning on a hostage situation.

My padmate had a razor

from dinner time

which never got collected.

So we sat down,

rolled a burn

and started chatting

about the situation ahead of us.

At first, like I said

it started off as a joke,

then things got out of hand.

It was me

who was to take my padmate hostage.

So I broke up the razor

and using my lighter,

I melted the blade

into the end of my pen.

Then I wrapped some sheet

around the bottom of the pen.

Then I was supposed to take him hostage
but he fluffed it at the last moment.
So I thought
it was supposed to end there.
But no, there was another twist
to the situation.

My padmate

came up with the idea

of me taking *myself* hostage.

At that time the idea sounded good,

as I was running on pure adrenalin.

I was up for anything.

So I sat down

with the blade in my right hand

and my padmate pressed the cell bell.

Three minutes later,

the night cloggy* came to our door

and asked us, "What's the emergency?"

To this my padmate replied,

"My padmate's got a blade to his throat

and I'm scared

in case he does anything."

* Also known as the night clockie, in some prisons.

The night cloggy told my padmate
that he would go and sort it out.

I then smashed up my pad,
to make the situation more real.

Then about six screws and a nurse

came to my door.

At first,

one of the screws tried to sweet talk me

into giving him the blade back.

So I told him to fuck off

and to suck his mum.

I don't know why

I told him to suck his mum,

because I think

that's a horrible thing to say.

After about five minutes,

two or three screws

had tried to make me

give the makeshift knife to them,

but me, being a stubborn bastard

as I am,

I was having none of it.

Then the nurse came and spoke to me
and I don't know what she was saying,
but she was proper upset
that I was holding myself hostage.

Then came the question,

"What do you want?"

I don't know what the fuck happened,

but I asked for a *dog*.

Of all things, to ask for a fucking dog!

I said, "If I come out of this pad,
I want a guarantee
that I won't be tweeked up
and taken down to unit 7"
(the punishment block).

They made the guarantee,
so I let them open the door,
chucked the knife on the floor
and kicked it out of the cell.
Then I had to come out of the cell
and be searched.

Then they said

I had to go up to the hospital wing

overnight.

Mind you, this was still only 9.15 p.m.

So I went up to the hospital wing

and I had to wait

for the doctor to come, in from the out.

So while I was waiting,

I sat and watched

the last fifteen minutes

of Man. United versus Bayern Munich.

Man. U. lost 2 - 1, so that gutted me.

Then I watched T.V. Nightmares 7.

Fucking well funny.

Then the doctor came.
I had to sit in the room
with two screws,
two nurses and a doctor
and I had to explain what was going on.
In the end, I was given medication
to help me sleep. It didn't help.
Eventually, I did fall asleep.

Next day I saw a different doctor.

He made a referral to the psychiatrist,

changed some of my medication

and I was screwing

because I got put on a 2052SH.

Absolutely screwing.

About 10 a.m.

I got taken back to my unit,

only to find out

I'm now not allowed a padmate

because they think I will hurt them.

I have now been on single bang up

for about three weeks

and I think it's great.

Cool*Books*

new fiction for adult learners in prison

A pioneering project in adult literacy for prisons, to create 6 new, original, adult readers specifically written and illustrated for and by offenders, plus the creation of a **Cool*Books*** DIY guide for use by any prison, to create further prison-specific reading materials.

This project has been devised and delivered by leading adult literacy publisher **Gatehouse Books** and the premier prison arts organisation **The Writers in Prison *Network*.**

Writers in Prison

The **Writers in Residence in Prison Scheme** was set up in 1992 by the Arts Council of England and the Home Office. Since that time 50 residencies have been placed in a wide variety of establishments throughout the country. It is run by the **Writers in Prison *Network*.**

The Scheme employs writers who are experienced or established in particular literary fields; many have been creative writing tutors or have worked in publishing, the theatre, television, radio or journalism. They are skilled communicators and facilitators with a genuine interest in working with the prison population.

The writers are there to enrich the whole prison, available to work with both staff and inmates. They have created a legacy of magazines, anthologies, reading groups, audio, video and live drama productions and other projects which have helped project a positive image for the prison. They have also brought into the prison writers and poets, theatre groups and musicians for staged events, readings and workshops.